Oh My, I Think I See Books

The Traveling Train

Nani

Happy Reading,
Hugs
Nani
xoxo

AuthorHouse™
1663 Liberty Drive
Bloomington, IN 47403
www.authorhouse.com
Phone: 1 (800) 839-8640

Published by AuthorHouse 10/18/2018

ISBN: 978-1-5462-5156-9 (sc)
ISBN: 978-1-5462-5155-2 (e)

Library of Congress Control Number: 2018908331

Print information available on the last page.

Any people depicted in stock imagery provided by Getty Images are models, and such images are being used for illustrative purposes only.
Certain stock imagery © Getty Images.

This book is printed on acid-free paper.

Because of the dynamic nature of the Internet, any web addresses or links contained in this book may have changed since publication and may no longer be valid. The views expressed in this work are solely those of the author and do not necessarily reflect the views of the publisher, and the publisher hereby disclaims any responsibility for them.

authorHOUSE®

To my husband, children, family and friends for their inspiration and constant love

Oh my, I think I see
a shiny new train rolling by me.

Clickety-clack, clickety-clack,
it rolls along the track.

The engine car is big and bold.
On its side is a star of gold.

The engine is the very first car.
The caboose is last, way off and far.

In the window, never taking a nap,
the engineer proudly wears his cap.

There are different trains with cars that go.
Some carry people and others haul cargo.

The engineer blows the horn–
people near the track are warned.

We all must stop at the railroad sign,
as the train speeds by to be on time.

8

If on a train you choose to go,
a ticket you've bought you'll need
to show.

Clickety-clack, clickety-clack,
it rolls along the track.

Smoke comes out of the stack, billowing around in black.

Some trains are short and some are long.
Count the cars as they roll along.

Train cars I count: one, two, three, four.
Could there be any more?

Yes, here comes the caboose in red,
with a moose whose name is Fred.

When the train has finished with its run,
the passengers get off to have some fun.

The cargo train unloads its haul,
which may be used to help us all.

TRAIN STATION

16

The train has passed; it's on its way along the countryside with bales of hay.

Away the train rolls up the hill.
Will we see it tomorrow? Yes, we will!

Clickety-clack, clickety-clack,
the Traveling Train is done.

You've learned so much and had such fun.

Which part was your favorite one?

Rhyming Words

see / me
clack / track
bold / gold
car / far
nap / cap
go / cargo
horn / warned
sign / time
go / show
stack / black
long / along
four / more
caboose / moose
red / Fred
run / fun
haul / all
way / hay
hill / will
done / fun / one

From our "Traveling Train" book, rhyming words galore. When you read the story again, you could find even more.

About the Writer

The writer, Nani (Linda Lodato Mortellaro) is a retired educator. She earned a Bachelors Degree in elementary education with a concentration in early childhood education . She also holds a Masters Degree in reading education and has worked as a classroom teacher, reading specialist, reading diagnostician and reading resource teacher for a county in her home state. She is also a lifetime Alumni Member of USF .

Nani and her husband have two grown accomplished children and in law children. The writer and her husband enjoy being with family and friends, traveling and of course, love children! The writer hopes to instill an appreciation of books and enjoyment of reading in preschool children!